Belinda Blinked 1;

A modern story of sex, erotica and passion;

How the sexiest sales girl in business earns her huge bonus by being the best at removing her high heels.

Author; Rocky Flintstone;

Cover Art; Mouldy Wood;

Chapters;

Chapter 1; The Job Interview

Chapter 2; The leather Room;

Chapter 3; The Regional Sales Meeting;

Chapter 4; The Maze;

Chapter 5; The First Client;

Chapter 6; The Second Client;

Chapter 7; The Third Client;

Chapter 8; The Tombola;

Chapter 9; The Chalet;

Chapter 10; The Horse and Jockey;

Chapter 11; Sunday Night 11.55pm;

Chapter 12; The Night Receptionist;

Chapter 13; The Duchess Comes Clean;

Chapter 14; Monday Morning 7.45am;

Chapter 1;

The Job Interview;

Belinda blinked, it wasn't a dream, the job interviewer had just asked her to remove her jacket and silk blouse. The Managing Director across the desk who had innocently brought her through from reception smiled and nodded at her. Slowly with the hint of a tease, Belinda removed the two garments. Her black brassiere was doing overtime to contain her full breasts, she had worn this one for today as it was tight fitting on purpose... she never thought it would be exposed in such a simple way.

The MD got up and took her blouse and jacket. He hung them onto one of two elegant wooden coat racks in the corner and sat back down. What next Belinda thought?
The interviewer resumed his questioning of her CV and after about five minutes, asked her to remove her knee length skirt. Belinda stood up, removed the offending garment and passed it with some surprise to the MD.

Underneath she was wearing a skimpy black thong and sexy black stockings which she didn't apologize for; after all she was an upmarket woman. She sat down again and crossed her long legs. She knew they looked good, but she really felt she wanted to keep her private pussy area hidden. Belinda leaned back on the white leather seat and started to gently sweat.

After a further ten minutes of questioning the MD got up and walked round to Belinda, he gently pulled her stockings down to her ankles. He removed her bright red high heels and stuffed the stockings inside them. They were placed under the coat rack by the interviewer. Belinda was now feeling exposed, with only a bra and thong left, she thought total nakedness was not far away, and then what?

The MD then surprised her by saying they wanted to offer her the job as their Sales Director today on completion of a few further details. Belinda was surprised as the job was worth £85,000 a year plus car and all the travel perks, so she nodded her head. With her agreement given the MD walked behind her and unhooked the tight black bra in a rapid movement. Belinda's breasts plunged to freedom and her nipples immediately stood to attention.

The MD sat down and appraised her, whilst the interviewer calmly asked her to stand up and remove her thong. Her shaven pussy was revealed with just a delicate runway of dark pubic hair guiding any viewer to the top of her vagina.

'Now sit down and relax Miss Blumenthal.' said the interviewer. 'In fact, just spread your legs wide so we can get a good look at your internal attributes.'
Belinda lay back in the leather chair and spread her legs wide as requested. Her vaginal lids popped open and her labial pinkness was there for them to assess. She quickly became moist and a runnel of liquid trickled down her left lower thigh.

The MD then said, 'My name is Tony, and you will report directly to me. Bill here is our Human Resources Director and he's available to you at all times. You might need him as you have a direct staff of 28, some of whom may need fucking off!

Belinda nodded and asked, which, was to her the obvious question, 'When are you guys going to fuck me?' Tony quickly replied, 'Well, Bill here never will as it's not in his area of responsibility, and I might, depending on how hard you work for me. But let's get to the point Belinda, the reason we've put you through this scenario is to ensure your positive reaction to certain members of our customer base who will definitely try you out. So I have to ask you here and now, does this give you any problems?'

Belinda blinked, shook her head and said, 'As long as I have your and the companies backing I will do whatever is necessary to make the sales happen.'
'Well done Belinda.' said Tony as a large smile crossed his rugged features.

Tony then dismissed Bill and said to him as he left the room,
'Send in Giselle with the contract.'

After a few minutes a 26 year old, stunningly attractive, blonde haired girl joined them with notebook and sheaf of papers in hand.
'Put the paperwork down Giselle and meet Belinda our new Sales Director.'
Belinda stood up, still totally naked and shook Giselle's hand. In response Giselle held Belinda's face in her hand and kissed her fully square on her lips, Belinda instinctively opened her mouth and Giselle's tongue snaked in and they both shared the touching of ecstasy.

At that magical moment Giselle started to strip off. It didn't take long as she wasn't wearing any underwear and Belinda thought, this girl does this too often for it to be a once in a lifetime event. However Giselle was a magnificent creature, tits that were to die for and an ass that was so tight, even Belinda felt tested, though she was equal in every respect and in all truth felt she had better shaped boobs. With soft deft actions, she soon had Belinda gasping. Belinda could only respond by sucking Giselle's breasts and teething her nipples vigorously. Not a bad final interview for the job of her dreams.

Chapter 2;

The Leather Room;

Three weeks later Belinda had settled into most of the administration parts of the job, but was still to get to grips with the large customer base and her new sales force. It was a typical wet dismal Thursday afternoon at the office and tomorrow, Friday was her first Regional sales meeting where she would discuss sales with her four regional managers. The town hall clock had just chimed three when Giselle called her to Tony's office.

'Afternoon Belinda.' said Tony, 'There's a very senior company event on Sunday at our chairman's country house, BBQ and all that. Wear tennis gear... very casual, no and I repeat no undergarments such as thongs or bra.'
Belinda looked up now intrigued. Tony smiled and said... 'You'll understand when you get there! I'll get Giselle to book you a room for Sunday night at the local hotel. It's called the Horse and Jockey. OK? It's probably best if you check in before you get to the old man's place.'

Belinda nodded, 'I can certainly rearrange my shopping trip to Saturday. Oh and I'll not bother purchasing any thongs or bras!' She smiled sweetly and Tony laughed.
'Good, go through to my leather room whilst I get Giselle'. Tony opened what looked like a normal cupboard door in the corner of his office and switched on some delicate lighting. Belinda went in and the door shut behind her.

'Wow!' she thought, Tony wasn't joking, this was her first visit to this part of the offices and the entire room including the floor was covered in exquisite leather tiles, they must have cost a fortune. There was no other furniture except an extremely sophisticated and expensive drinks cabinet in the corner.
'What does he get up to in here?' she thought.

Belinda realized that she might find out sooner than she bargained for. Anyway, what did it matter, she had been surprised that he hadn't come onto her since that final interview. After all he was a good looking single guy and was very professional in his approach to the business. With his astute guidance she had successfully installed herself as Sales Director and was now preparing her strategy on some major accounts, again with his help.

Belinda thought about Giselle, she was probably Tony's preferred taste in women, five years younger than herself at 24, Giselle was blonde not dark like Belinda, She was Tony's PA and right hand man, foreign, of Dutch nationality, and probably the successor to Tony as MD in four or five years when Tony moved up in the company hierarchy. Belinda was not interested in becoming MD so no conflict would ever exist between her and Giselle. This was probably a good thing for her longevity with the outfit.

Belinda's thoughts were interrupted when the door opened and Giselle walked in.
'Hi Belinda, what do you think of his "fucking leather room"?'

Belinda smiled and said, 'I could do with a drink….'

Giselle walked over to the drinks cabinet, poured two stiff Gin and Tonics and started to stroke Belinda's tits with her long fingernails. Belinda felt herself respond and took a swift drink while she still could. Unasked she put her tongue into Giselle's mouth.

'That tastes good' said Giselle as she removed Belinda's jacket and skirt. Belinda slipped the straps of Giselle's dress down her arms and in a swift movement removed the whole dress. 'Very professional Belinda.' said Giselle as she again turned her attention to Belinda's tits. It only took Giselle a second to remove Belinda's satin blouse and push up her bra cups. Belinda's nipples started to swell in anticipation before Giselle's lips and teeth started to punish them.

It took about as much time for Belinda to unhook Giselle's bra and then slip her knickers to the floor. Giselle deftly stepped out of them and kicked her heels to the side of the room. 'Lie down on the floor Belinda, and enjoy all that leather.' said the now completely naked Giselle.

Belinda did as she was told as well as pulling off her bra. Now stretched out on the floor with only her thong in place Belinda was game for anything… besides what else would she be doing on a wet Thursday afternoon, twelve hours before her first Regional Sales meeting?

Giselle's hands soon made light work of Belinda's thong. The two girls started to excite each other and soon their respective vaginas were wet and steaming. They took it in turns to lick each other's clits and when Tony entered the room they were both ready for a bit of male interaction.

However Tony had other ideas and just brushed Belinda's body with his hands feeling her responsive breasts and ass. His real objective was Giselle and pretty soon he was deeply into licking her pussy. Meanwhile Giselle was doing the same to Belinda so all in all everyone was getting satisfaction. After about fifteen minutes of this intense activity Belinda excused herself, gathered together her discarded clothes and let herself out of the leather room. Giselle and Tony stayed on for an extra session which Giselle would no doubt enlighten Belinda about at Friday lunch.

Whilst starting to dress in Tony's office the main receptionist Bella walked in and caught Belinda naked adjusting her thong. 'Here, let me do that for you,' said Bella, 'I know how important it is to achieve a straight line with a thong…. look at mine.' Bella hitched up her dress and revealed an even more skimpy thong than Belinda was wearing. Belinda stroked Bella's ass in appreciation and thought the obvious… not another one! What is this office running on… high powered sexual adrenelin?

Bella turned round and caressed Belinda's substantial tits which were still suffering from Giselle's attentions. Belinda responded by putting her hand between Bella's legs, pushing Bella's thong to one side so she could finger her clit. Bella groaned and started kissing Belinda's mouth.

'Help me dress' gasped Belinda, not wanting to be discovered by Tony and Giselle exiting the leather room, which Bella had probably no idea existed. Bella took the hint and calmed down, taking inordinate pleasure in placing Belinda's bra and stockings onto her smooth body.

Let's do this again and in private.' said Belinda. Bella nodded whilst straightening Belinda's thong for the last time and picked up the correspondence she had gone to Tony's office to collect for the last post.

I'll hold you to that Belinda,' said Bella, 'My place next Friday evening, say 9.00pm.'
It's a date!' Belinda replied, wondering how she'd have the sexual strength to get through the next week, but instinctively she knew if sex was made available then she'd take it all in good stead.

Belinda went to her office and picked up her briefcase. On the desk was an agenda with client attendance details of the Sunday bash at the Chairman's house. It would make interesting reading that night when she got back to her apartment as well as the final preparations for her Regional Sales Manager meeting in the morning. Outside in the car park Belinda jumped into her two week old Mercedes coupe. Swish and expensive, Belinda so loved this part of the job. She gunned the engine and drove the twenty minutes to her new central London apartment.

Chapter 3;

The Regional Sales Meeting;

Belinda had an early breakfast and was in the office for 07.30am. This was probably a pretty important day for her as it would be the first time she would meet her UK senior sales management, in other words the people who reported to her in business terms. She had no particular views... just lots of third party information about the performance and caliber of these four managers. There were also twenty or so salesmen who reported to them on the ground and she had fairly, or unfairly, pessimistic thoughts about how the whole sales organization was performing.

But in sales you can always be surprised, especially when you talked to people in confidence and got them on board... to accept your way of doing things. Belinda was good at this, and Tony knew it... this was probably one of the many reasons he had hired her. There was no major desire in Tony's business plan to sack all the sales force and bring in new people... develop what we have was his mantra.

Belinda had already thrashed out a strategy with Tony in her first three weeks of induction to the company... it was simple, if the salesmen and sales managers show any sign of performance then keep them. If not, bite the bullet and dispose. Belinda was tough but not mercenary and she would use all her talents to make the existing sales team work. She just wondered how far she would have to go to get them onside.

Nine-o-clock came and Bella rang her from reception to say the two northerly Regional managers wanted a lift from Heathrow as they couldn't get a taxi to take them to the offices. Classic, Belinda thought, the company locates near Heathrow and you can't get a taxi between the two places as the taxi fare is too low! Belinda picked up the phone to her Sales administration manager, Jim Thompson... her Mr. Fix It in the sales organization. 'Hi Jim, Belinda here, can you rescue my two Regional Sales Managers from the Airport?'

'Be delighted to Belinda, can I take the pool car?' replied Jim.

'Sure,' Belinda replied, 'Just put the cost centre to both of them!'

Jim laughed heartily and said, 'Will do!'

A knock on Belinda's door saw her London and Home Counties Regional Sales Manager stick his head around the door. 'Pardon the intrusion Ms. Blumenthal, but I'm Des Martin... you know, your London man.'

Belinda got up, 'Des! Great to meet you, grab a seat, we're just picking two of the guys up from Heathrow, which only leaves our man from the West to appear.'

'Ah, you mean Dave Wilcox from Bristol.' said Des.

'I certainly do.' replied Belinda as she sat down behind her desk. 'Oh by the way, call me Belinda from now on.'

'Will do Belinda.' replied Des confidently as he eyed her shapely legs and ass.

Belinda thought, 'I like you Des Martin, confident, sophisticated, good looking, but why the terrible sales performance?' She sighed and leaned back in her chair pushing forward her breasts. 'So Des are you prepared for today? Are you ready to expose yourself, your team and your client base to the new lady and master?'

'Belinda,' said Des, 'If I'm honest it will be the first time anyone in this company has taken an interest in us salesmen instead of bypassing us with corporate deals done from head office over a bottle of whisky.'

Belinda looked shocked, 'Tell me you're joking... is this the real story I'm about to find out about today?''

'Put it this way,' said Des, 'you can't say I didn't warn you!' He also thought what a magnificent pair of tits, how long will it take me to get them into my hands and is my job worth it?

A second knock at her office door saw the Western Regional Sales Manager, Dave Wilcox, pop his head around. 'Hope I'm not late, but the traffic on the M4 was desperate!'

'Come on in Dave, I'm Belinda and very nice to meet you!'

Minutes later Jim Thompson rang and told Belinda the two other Regional Sales Managers would be in the car park in three minutes. 'Thanks Jim, get them up to the conference room ASAP and we'll get started for 10.00am.'

The conference room was upmarket, Tony liked to impress those customers who visited the offices and one of the best ways was decent meeting spaces. Jim quickly introduced Patrick

O'Hamlin, the Scottish and Ireland Regional Sales Manager and Ken Dewsbury, Regional Sales manager for Central and North England. Both were like chalk and cheese... Patrick was a fast talking Irishman, originally born in Dublin, whilst Ken was from God's own country, South Yorkshire, and sported an accent to match.

'My God,' thought Belinda, 'What a varied team, surely we can do something with this lot.'

Belinda called the meeting to a halt at noon. Patrick and Dave had each given their hourly presentation, though Belinda could have asked enough questions to extend their presentations to three hours each. However she knew she needed an overview, and the detail could come later in the field when she spent time with each manager individually. Lunch was a quick pint and sandwich in the local pub... The Bull in the Rushes, and as time was of the essence she felt she could only work a little bit of her female magic.

In the ladies toilets, Belinda removed her jacket, blouse and bra, she ran the cold tap and dabbed the water onto her nipples, making them stand to attention. 'That'll have to do for now she thought as she shoved her bra into her leather handbag. She put her blouse back on leaving three of the five buttons undone. She was now showing her cleavage big time and threw her jacket casually over her shoulder. The silken blouse quickly became transparent due to the water and clung longingly to her stunning breasts.

She walked back into the drinking area and observed the effect she had on her new sales team. Only two of her Managers immediately observed her subtle change of attire, and Belinda soon noticed some astute elbowing going around the team, accompanied with wry smiles from the Northerners. Jim was chuckling to himself as he was office based and had heard the rumours put around by Bella and Giselle. Now he could believe them.

The afternoon sessions were equally as professional and Belinda was particularly impressed by Ken Dewsbury, the man showed wit, style and competence in that order. Des Martin was however a true pro, his London bearing and obvious sales talents indicated to Belinda that he was probably her first avenue to finding out how the individual members of the regional sales team ticked.

By the end of the meeting Belinda's blouse had dried out, but her lack of bra and hardened nipples chaffing continually against her tight blouse were still being noticed. Good she thought, let's see who has the guts to make the first move. In her short closing comments which wound down the business side of things, Belinda suggested they all adjourn to the Pentra Hotel which was beside Heathrow airport. That meant the two managers who were on evening flights to Leeds and Glasgow could get off easily and the rest of them could drive home after the rush hour traffic.

Belinda also decided to throw in a couple of wild cards so she asked Giselle and Bella if they would join her team for a couple of drinks on their way home. Both were as keen as mustard when they found out it was all on Belinda's expenses. Jim Thompson drove the three girls over to the Pentra where they met the Regional Sales Managers in the "Long bar" which overlooked the runway. It was now six o clock and the bar was filling up. Jim found seats at a table tucked away in the far corner of the room.

Belinda started the proceedings by taking off her jacket and downing her G&T in one. Bella followed and Giselle "accidently" spilt some of her drink over her blouse, which meant she had to go to the restroom to dry off. In fact, all that came off was her bra and like Belinda earlier that day, she was ready for action with a translucent white blouse and to die for nipples. Jim was on the ball and by the time Giselle had returned he had two replacement G&T's on the table. Bella by now had gathered the "drift" of the drinks session and decided to do her bit for team building. As she wasn't wearing a bra that day she coyly unbuttoned the top three of her blouse buttons and slowly removed her jacket.

Her cleavage was revealed and a quiet gasp of admiration went around the table. Giselle flicked some tonic water at Bella's nipples and soon achieved the desired result. 'Take it off Bella.' Des Martin whispered...'the tonic will stain your blouse... look at Belinda's and Giselle's already!'

Bella smiled and thought, 'Will I be the first? Surely Belinda can't as these guys report to her. Then in a quick movement Bella unbuttoned the rest of her blouse and let her magnificent breasts hang out for all to see.

Ken Dewsbury choked over his pint of bitter whilst the other three Regional Managers chanted quietly, 'Who's next! Who's next!' Belinda looked at Giselle who nodded and in a leisurely fashion with a big hint of tease unbuttoned the rest of her blouse. Her tits hung freely like pomegranates and she gently massaged them with her hands. 'Come on Belinda!' whispered Ken, ''Don't let the sales team down now!'

Belinda smiled, and replied, 'I'll want a 10% increase in your sales next month Ken!'

'Done!' he replied.

Belinda slowly opened the remaining two buttons of her blouse, her tits fell loose, she took a drink and started to massage her nipples with her fingertips. The RSM's all clapped in admiration. Never had they had a sales meeting culminate like this one, things were looking up, and with three pairs of stunning breasts on show, they could do anything.

Jim Thompson went to get more drinks and the girls started to finger and discuss the merits of each other's nipples.

'Don't make us more jealous girls.' said Patrick O'Hamlin, 'but I've got a plane to catch!'

'Me too!' said Ken Dewsbury. They both got up, shook everyone's hands and departed with much looking over their shoulders at the line up of tit available at the table. How they wished they both had the guts to finger those breasts.

The bar was now getting more crowded and Belinda thought it was sensible to button up their blouses, as they didn't want to get accused of being prostitutes. Des Martin and Dave Wilcox drank up, sadly said their goodbyes and disappeared out of the bar.

'Thanks Donna and Giselle you really helped me make a breast of it!' said Belinda laughing. 'One more drink and Jim will get us back to the office.' Jim went back to the bar ordered the drinks and paid the tab. The girls drank up slowly, reliving the looks on each of the Regional Managers faces when they showed them their breasts.

'That was interesting Belinda,' said Donna, 'Any more events like that for us?'

'Let's wait and see,' replied Belinda, 'Let's wait and see!'

Chapter 4;

The Maze;

Saturday morning came all too quickly and was bright and breezy, but dry, ideal for a quick game of tennis and then later a spot of shopping and browsing through the cook shops of London's Oxford Street. Belinda thought it was important to not only know her own brand but also those of the opposition. That evening she planned to do an internet search on the guest list for tomorrow's function where she would be unable to wear bra or thong... definitely a strange request.

Sunday morning was warm so Belinda put the soft top down and motored over to Windsor. True to her instructions she checked into the Horse and Jockey and removed her inner clothing. Now dressed in only her tennis gear she drove to the Chairman's house. She parked next to Tony's car and jumped into his passenger seat.

'Good morning Tony.' Her tennis skirt had risen up to show the top of her thighs. Tony pulled it up at the front and studied her pussy. He then pulled up her tennis shirt and inspected her tits.

Hi Belinda, good to see you're good to go, so lets quickly go through the guest list and discuss our targets with their potential. After we've done this we'll get some lunch and take up our positions.

'So I can readjust my clothing Tony?' Belinda blinked. 'Or do you want me to parade to lunch like this?'

Forty minutes later after some food and two strong gin and tonics, Tony took her to a medium sized garden maze located at the rear of the property. They entered the tall undergrowth and Tony led her through it without a pause. Belinda was glad someone knew their way through the myriad of paths and openings. After three minutes they entered a glade which was obviously the central point of the maze. He pushed Belinda's back onto a flimsy wooden trellis, gave her a quick kiss and attached her arms to the trellis with a set of red plastic handcuffs attached to a length of parcel string. Belinda was now thoroughly intrigued and a little excited at what was about to happen and laughed out loud, 'Tony, how did you know my favourite handcuff colour was red? Seriously though, I've not seen a pair of these since my days in Kindergarten!'

Tony smiled as he backed away from Belinda.

'Tony... what's going on?' said Belinda now seriously trying to control her amusement.

'Trust me Belinda, treat your clients well and let's see the business roll in. I'll return and "release" you in under two hours. Keep your chin up and let your tits and clit do the talking!' With these erotic words ringing in her ears, Tony walked off.

The grass underfoot felt wet and Belinda could hear a sprinkler nearby which kept wetting her ankles, the area of wet grass would soon become a mud patch she thought... how disgusting. She hated mud at the best of times, but tied to this garden fence meant she couldn't move around... much, it would soon get really muddy and quickly.

Her thoughts were interrupted by the sound of cheerful whistling coming down the maze. Ahh, here's my first client she thought.
Alfonse Stirbacker from Belgium strolled into the glade and studied Belinda's position with obvious interest. From Tony's outline and her internet research, Belinda recognized him and his potential immediately...over 300 supermarket outlets throughout Belgium, Northern France and Southern Holland and they were soon to push into the UK.
'A good start.' she thought.

Chapter 5;

The First Client;

Alfonse Stirbacker;

'Good afternoon young lady, and who do I have the pleasure of meeting, albeit in this strange situation?'

'Hi Mr Stirbacker, my name is Belinda Blumenthal and I'm the Sales Director of Steele Pots and Pans. She always felt she should apologise for the terrible company name, but she also knew it was so awful that very few people ever forgot it.
Stirbacker replied, 'Excellent, you look like my type of girl… young, dark and mysterious! As you know my name you will also know I am the purchasing director of my company. Let's get to know each other, we have only 20 minutes contact, and I intend to make full use of them.

Alfonse immediately got to work by removing his one garment of a black thong and taking off Belinda's shoes and socks. Completely naked he pushed up her white shirt partially uncovering her breasts. He then pulled her tennis skirt down to her knees and backed off. How strange Belinda thought… he's just a voyeur… he doesn't want any close contact. Maybe he's happily married?

Alfonse then said to Belinda, 'Would you visit me in my offices in Brussels and let me see your body again? Perhaps I could see more of it, and possibly in a less disgusting environment. Belinda immediately understood, Alfonse needed order and homely comforts in order to progress his male desires, though his cock had quickly become completely erect. She replied, 'Absolutely Mr Stirbacker I'm so glad I fit your expectations, and I would really like to do a lot of business with you'.

Stirbacker grinned and said, 'That is assured my lovely Belinda, and he fondled her waiting tits with relish. Belinda groaned softly, one of his hands slipped down to her vagina and started to gently caress it. In return she stroked his penis with both hands.

'A gentleman from Brussels thought Belinda, what a great start to the afternoon!' After a further ten minutes of extremely heavy fondling, Belinda was becoming very wet, Alfonse had now gotten to her tits big time with his teeth and his very long cock had penetrated her vulva. He was obviously enjoying her tits and clit as Tony had put it so aptly just fifteen minutes earlier, and she had her first major client breakthrough. She mentally penciled in a visit to Brussels in ten days time. No sense in not striking whilst the iron was hot… so to speak!

A far off whistle sounded and Alfonse backed off… 'Time for me to go Belinda, I thoroughly enjoyed your lack of bra and thong… very thoughtful, but don't forget them when you visit me in Brussels very soon. We will have dinner at my very exclusive gentleman's club and all our ladies are expected to be properly dressed... at least when they arrive!

Belinda replied, 'Don't worry Mr Stirbacker I'll be in touch very soon!

Chapter 6;

The Second Client;

Jim Stirling.

A few minutes after Alfonse had gone Belinda heard her second visitor stomping through the maze. He appeared a few seconds later, again dressed only in a black thong. It was becoming a type of uniform she thought. From the guest list info Belinda recognized Jim Stirling, a Yankee from the USA. His operation had 1257 outlets and was also growing fast in Mexico and Brazil. He was a big guy but short, and upon seeing Belinda's plight quickly threw his somewhat stained thong to the ground.

Belinda blinked;
For the first time that day she was caught unawares... there was nothing there, but then she saw it, underneath covered in pubic hairs lay a very small and in Belinda terms, somewhat pathetic penis. Belinda gasped, what was she expected to do with this?

'Hi, my name's Stirling, from the US. Let's get these garments out of the way!'
With one powerful movement he ripped Belinda's tennis shirt completely from her body, and seconds later had done the same to her skirt. He flung them to the ground where they now lay ruined in the mud.
'Hope you don't mind Missy as I likes 'em bare!' Jim didn't hang around and immediately took her tits in his massive hands. His large thumbs tentatively rubbed her nipple tips, making them rise and harden. This fast reaction from Belinda seemed to please him and he started to push his cock into her vagina.

Belinda squatted slightly as Jim was shorter than her, pulling her legs apart to allow him easier access. Jim grunted and Belinda thought she felt something entering her pussy. He started to fuck her hard, Belinda breathed deeply, did the man know he was only tickling her? , This was going to take all her concentration, Stirling's was a massive account and if she did well today, who knew what might develop from it. He started to press her harder and harder against the trellis, he had found his rhythm but Belinda couldn't feel anything and whilst she had the appetite for it she knew she would have to fake it and Belinda never faked anything. To make matters worse the ground was now really boggy and her torn garments were well and truly stained.

Belinda thought of delicious sexual scenarios and succeeded in making her vagina become wetter and wetter. She started to slowly contract her cervical muscles to ensure Jim got the friction he needed to complete his ejaculation. After ten minutes of hard work he came and then started to lick her tits. He obviously had little regard for women as he then pushed her head down to his cock ensuring Belinda's long black hair fell nearly to the by now muddy ground, her ample breasts followed and Stirling pushed his penis into her mouth. Belinda smiled to herself, she could have eaten two of these for breakfast, never mind the scrambled eggs.

Just then she heard the whistle and she knew she had done her best. Stirling reluctantly let go of her tits and put his thong back on... it was now even more stained than when he had entered the maze and Belinda wondered where all the semen had come from. Perhaps she had underestimated his resources?

'Hey babe, what's your name?' said Stirling.

'Belinda Blumenthal, I'm the Sales Director of Steele Pots and Pans.'

'Good work Belinda, come and see me in Texas in a couple of weeks... I need a new cookery utensil supplier and I guess you fit the bill!

'Why Jim, I'd love to... let's say in three weeks time?

'Yup... let's do it... and I promise to replace your soiled garments with something a little bit more sexy!'

With that he stumped off leaving Belinda completely naked, very muddy and still tied to the trellis around the maze. She massaged her wrists where the red plastic handcuffs had managed to keep her attached to the trellis and thought of the bonus money she would personally make when she tied up the deal with Jim Stirling. She also thought she should take a crash course in Yoga, or some sort of exercises which developed the cervix muscles. If Jim couldn't rise to the job then she would have to ensure he was completely satisfied... the things she did to make her fortune!

But wait, she could hear another client approaching through the maze. 'Oh no,' she thought, 'I hope this one's a bit better hung, I can't take much more of these small appendages.' But she had to... the handcuffs and parcel string ensured it!

Chapter 7;

The Third Client;

Peter Rouse.

Belinda stood her ground hoping this one would be so much better, she had had enough titillation, she wanted, no, needed a good fuck. A tall blonde haired man, with an impressive physique strolled into view. Belinda quickly recognised Peter Rouse, his operation was located in Holland with 357 retail outlets, and again was growing strongly throughout the Scandinavian countries. An evasive entrepreneur, Peter could not be overlooked as he had recently expanded to Spain and Portugal. On seeing Belinda he quickly removed his thong and threw it to the ground whilst approaching her.

'My name is Peter,' he said and quickly bowed, 'I believe you are Belinda, the Sales Director of this fantastic customer bash your superiors are putting on here today!'
'Why yes I am Mr. Rouse.' said Belinda, blushing at her naked appearance in front of this, so far, delightfully hung man. After all, he was the first to know who she was.

'Please, please call me Peter,' he replied, 'especially as we are to become more intimately acquainted in the next 25 minutes.' He took Belinda's hands and said, 'What a delightful body you have, may I handle it?'
Belinda replied, 'Why yes of course... I would love to feel you touch me, feel as free as you wish.'
'Now that's an offer I cannot refuse,' Peter replied and immediately started to massage her neck, slowly spreading to her breasts and buttocks. Belinda immediately started to relax and responded by gently massaging Peter's penis.

He had a fantastic body and his muscles were very well toned, Belinda started to caress his body and in return he moved his massage to her vaginal area. He stroked her small runway of pubic black hair leading to her vaginal lips, and soon he was inside her with his fingers. Belinda had rarely experienced anything as delicate as this and soon began to moan softly. In return she still had the sense of presence to massage his now extremely hard and large penis. She somehow knew she was going to enjoy this man.

After a few moments Peter pushed Belinda onto her knees, into the soft mud and gently guided her head to his penis. Belinda opened her mouth and slowly pushed her lips over his foreskin, pulling it back before slightly gagging as she swallowed his entire cock down her throat. 'You are very skilful Belinda, would you let me teach you more techniques?'
'Why yes Peter I always love to learn new things.'

He then lifted her from the ground and slowly penetrated her vagina with his now throbbing cock. Belinda again moaned softly...his penetration was so fluid she felt in ecstasy. He started to move inside her, she responded by contracting and releasing her vaginal muscles in time to his thrusts. They were now completely intertwined, Belinda had never experienced anything like this before, she was floating on air and Peter was penetrating deeper and deeper. Belinda started to gasp in short spasms, she needed more and more oxygen just to feed the gigantic orgasm she was about to encounter. For the first time in her life she was not in control, but she was enjoying it to death.

Peter started to sweat profusely, Belinda started to rub his skin more vigorously and he approached his climax. Of course Belinda was now wild with delirium, she was completely out of her head, all her actions were mechanical, Peter kept thrusting, Belinda kept flexing her vaginal muscles, until they both came in a violent explosion of ecstasy together. Peter fell out of her, Belinda collapsed onto her knees in the mud... the plastic handcuffs around her wrists saving her from being completely immersed. Now on her knees she was spattered all over with the horrible slime, and there was nothing she could do about it... except linger in the fantastic orgasm she had just experienced.

But Peter's cock remained erect and Belinda was so impressed with his skills, she knew she could learn much more from him. So she crawled back to him and put her mouth over his penis and continued to screw him with her lips, teeth, tongue and throat... she secretly knew she was ready to become his sex slave if he would ask her. She would scream for more until he agreed she thought.

But Peter Rouse was no normal individual and he knew when a girl was under his sexual spell as Belinda now was, so he let her screw his penis in her mouth and began using the mud to mark Belinda's tits, ass, mouth, and ears with symbolic signs. She was still kneeling on the ground so he took the opportunity to write more symbols on her back which would bind her to him sexually for the next year.

His cock then started to ejaculate semen which he quickly caught in his hands. He then covered her hair with it, twisting it all into a ponytail, Belinda's long black hair mixed with translucent sperm... the most powerful sexual symbol he knew. Belinda, though she didn't know it, was now well and truly ensnared, though truth be told it was what Belinda would have wanted.

The whistle brought them both back to the present day, Peter hurriedly put on his thong whilst Belinda tried to get rid of some of the mud she was now covered in. Belinda gasped, 'When can I see you next Peter.... please.' she said desperately. 'Hush my beautiful Belinda, I will see you tonight at 11.30pm in the Horse and Jockey pub, where I know you have a room we can use.' Belinda smiled her gratitude to him and said, 'It will be so good... I promise you... ask anything you want... I somehow feel enslaved to you.'
'You are Belinda, as I am to you.' replied Peter. 'Until tonight!'

Chapter 8;

The Tombola;

Belinda was now both exhausted and exhilarated, she had been fucked by three males...
well let's be honest... two and a half, in the last two hours and had been totally mesmerized
by one of them. She also had a sixth sense that she could never opt out of the special
relationship Peter Rouse and herself had developed in their short meeting. But for all that
she was completely up for it, Peter was a successful, dominating character... and come to
think of it, so was she.

Now relaxing against the trellis she pulled the parcel string sharply and it fell to the muddy
ground. She slowly twisted the plastic handcuffs, they fell apart and she bent down to pick
up her tennis outfit. It was a real mess, but for decency's sake she put what was left of the
shirt and dress back on. She knew Tony would be here any minute to bring her back to the
BBQ area and then she could get back to her lovely bath at her room in the Horse and
Jockey. Soon she heard footsteps coming through the maze and thankfully it was Tony, he
had a large smile on his face.

'You're a star Belinda, those three guys you just entertained are over the moon with you...
and the other girls have done good as well.'
'What do you mean other girls?'
'Didn't you know? Giselle and Bella are here as well, it's not just you... it's your glee team as
well!'
'Tony! What do you mean by "glee team" we're all just girls out for a good time and I need a
bath!'

Tony looked at her and decided not to comment on her condition...he had never seen so
much mud stick to a person and what were those symbolic marks on her face and thighs?

They soon reached the BBQ area which had been transformed into a Roman style
amphitheater with over 40 people sitting around on chairs. They were mostly clients with
their wives who had up to this point no knowledge of the sexual adventures which a few of
their number had been allowed access to. Belinda sat down on a chair which Tony had
found for her. She looked around and tried to locate Giselle and Bella.

Belinda gasped when she recognised Giselle, her beautiful blonde hair had been, to say the
best, remodeled, by perhaps a maniac with a twist for the dramatic??? Her dress had seen
as much wear as Belinda's tennis outfit and was being held together by a few safety pins.
Giselle looked up and saw Belinda staring at her, she smiled and stared back at Belinda's
equally disgusting condition and torn clothing. Belinda thought perhaps she had gotten off
lightly, but why was Tony so happy, Giselle was his girl and she seemed to be in a bit of a
state. Belinda gave Giselle the thumbs up and looked around for Bella.

She soon spotted her and to be honest Bella didn't look that much better than Giselle, though her hair was intact, her outfit was sporting half a dozen safety pins. Bella's face was however covered in red lipstick as though another maniac had tried to apply it. They had definitely succeeded in making her look like a tart. Belinda caught Bella's eye and smiled at her. Bella gave her the thumbs up and smiled back.

Belinda thought, 'This is very strange, what's going to happen next?'
A couple of minutes later a tall chap stood up and addressed the gathering.
'Welcome everyone to our annual Tombola where our prizes are the same as previous years. I also want to personally thank Sir James Godwin for letting us have this opportunity to raise some much needed money for our local charity, The Asses & Donkeys Trust. Now, please remember as your prize is a real person you will only get your servant for the time period of 12 hours. The highest bidder from this audience for each individual prize gets to take them home!' The audience clapped enthusiastically.

The tall man continued, 'There is also only one rule, and that is we have a safe word, which when uttered means the owner stops the directed task right away and the servant is released from their 12 hour duty. The down side of that is, the servant has to match the donation paid by the bidder to our charity! We all win! OK! Yes, now please remember girls and potential owners the safe word is THIMBLE, yes thimble... easy to remember, it stops you from getting pricked!! Ha ha!' The crowd groaned and started clapping.

Belinda blinked; she was intrigued, this sounds like great fun. She quickly thought, 'Who would I pick as my prize... Tony?... Bella?... no, Sir James Godwin and boy would I enjoy that scenario.'

'Today we have three servants on offer and to find out who they are, and take note it could be any one of you here, I want you all to look under your chairs and see the number attached to it.' The sound of hurriedly scraping chairs filled the air whilst the now hushed audience checked their numbers. Belinda's was 13, 'Unlucky for some.' she thought.

'Ok,' the tall man shouted, 'let's tumble the tombola and see what the three "lucky" numbers are.' The tombola went round and round, Belinda felt a sense of adventure take over her persona, she somehow felt she knew she would be a prize, but she didn't know who would be her owner.

'The first number is 22, I repeat 22, would the person sitting on chair number 22 please stand up.' Belinda looked around to see who the lucky person was. It was Giselle and as she stood up a safety pin fell out revealing a beautiful right breast to the crowd. An appreciative murmur came from the men, which saw many of their wives elbowing them in the ribs. Did they dare bid for her after that Belinda thought?

'The second number is 37, I repeat 37.'
Bella stood up, her safety pins held and Belinda started to smell a rat.
'The third number is, unlucky for some, 13, I repeat number 13.'
Belinda jumped to her feet, ready to go, wondering who she would be a servant to for the next twelve hours. Her torn shirt fell wide apart revealing her breasts and her tennis skirt

flapped wide in the mounting breeze revealing her pubic hairline to the assembled body, but she didn't care, she was Belinda and she was going to make sure a big butch man took her home!

'Now,' said the tall man, 'This is where we make some money for our charity as the rest of you can bid for their services, but firstly, do I have the agreement of these three very fine ladies to be coerced into these important roles?'
Belinda thought, 'What the fuck, this might be fun… it's probably just doing a bit of cleaning and lawn mowing on a Sunday evening.'
She shouted out, 'Yes I'm game!' whilst covering up her private parts with her hands and arms.
The other two girls followed suit and happily agreed, the tall man bowed to them.
'Thank you for your noble assistance, our charity The Asses & Donkeys Trust is much indebted to you.' he said.

The bidding quickly started with Bella and she soon went for £350 to the American Jim Stirling who Belinda thought could do with a cock transplant, and very soon at that. Giselle went next for £300 from Tony of all people, definitely a case of protecting his own. Then it was Belinda's turn. The bids started slowly, and Belinda couldn't believe her body was that bad… perhaps it was all the mud… where was her butch man? Finally she went for £200 from a lady dressed in a white linen trouser suit and a panama hat called only the Duchess.

With Belinda sold, the tombola was over and the three girls were taken away to start their twelve hours of duty. The now devastated Belinda was immediately led to a hosepipe near the stables where the Duchess striped her of her torn skirt and tennis shirt and hosed her down. She roughly fondled Belinda's tits and ass in the washing process with a long handled brush and then pushed her, still naked, into a horsebox. With the rear tail gate down it was obvious that it all had been planned in advance, instead of straw and manure there was a sofa and drinks, albeit chilled, tinned Gin and Tonics.

The Duchess rudely pushed Belinda onto the sofa and offered her a drink. Belinda nervously poured the can down her by now parched throat, she was still feeling horny and didn't think her new owner could give her what she still craved even after the afternoons events. Quite a lot of the can didn't get down Belinda's throat and she made sure the liquid trickled down her neck onto her breasts and then into her tummy button where it pooled, overflowed and ran down her track of black pubic hair into her vagina.

Much to Belinda's surprise the Duchess murmured, 'Waste not, want not,' and promptly licked the gin off Belinda's tits, stomach and clitoris.

Belinda thought "Result!" but said nothing and let the Duchess enjoy her slurping hoping this was setting the tone for the rest of the evening. She asked for another G&T and this time the Duchess decided to pour it down Belinda's throat herself. It was obvious the Duchess was enjoying this relationship, as she cupped her free hand around Belinda's left breast whilst carelessly slopping the drink into her mouth.

'Had enough servant?' said the Duchess, 'as we have to move on or Sir James will be joining our little party!' The Duchess efficiently closed the tail door of the horse trailer to the chagrin of the quickly assembled party of stable lads, leaving Belinda reclining on the sofa and helping herself to another Gin and Tonic in comfort. It was just as well she could stretch out because the Duchess was not a competent driver of the large four wheel drive vehicle plus trailer. Belinda lost count of the cut corners and sudden halts as they drove through the country lanes to an exclusive Motel which had some private chalets in the grounds. Belinda wickedly hoped the Duchess was better at fucking than driving... or had a companion who could do both.

Chapter 9;

The Chalet;

Belinda felt the horse box reversing accompanied with the grinding of gears and then the engine of the four by four went dead. There was a silence for at least thirty minutes and Belinda started to feel abandoned. Then suddenly the tail gate opened and the Duchess climbed up the ramp. She was dressed in full horse riding gear, a red jacket, white jodhpurs, black boots, black jumping hat and crop with a scarlet tag on the end. Belinda blinked fearing the worst.

The Duchess grabbed Belinda's ass and pulled her up to a standing position. She then pushed her down the ramp and pulled her by her left tit into a chalet style building. The Duchess made for a doorway at the end of the lounge which led to a large wet room. She stood Belinda under the shower and turned it on. Slowly the Duchess started to strip off her riding gear in front of Belinda. Like Belinda the Duchess was well endowed, but her ass was showing signs of her 50 something years, and childbirth had not been kind to her stomach muscles. However she was still in good shape and the riding clothes had made the most of her attributes. Belinda could not help but hope she would not be in worse shape when she reached the same age, albeit some twenty years away!

Now totally naked the Duchess started to wash Belinda and herself down with shampoo and smelly natural oils. Belinda whispered a word of thanks for this thoughtful act, even though the Duchess's hands were all over her vagina, ass and breasts. The Duchess immediately frowned and stepped out of the shower area to pick up her crop which was laid close to hand across the wash hand basin.
'Address me as "My Lady" and nothing else!' and to emphasize this she flicked the crop onto the cheek of Belinda's right ass. The crop's impact made Belinda jump and left a nasty bright red mark on her skin. Belinda grimaced and replied quickly,
'Thank you My Lady.'
'That's better servant.' said the Duchess.

The Duchess set the crop aside and continued to wash down Belinda, again applying plenty of hand squeezing to her tits. After five minutes of this the Duchess changed her tactics and concentrated on her vagina and clitoris. Belinda's nipples started to respond, she was after all, that type of girl and couldn't help it. However, the Duchess started to smile and said,
'That's very good servant.'
'Thank you My Lady.' replied Belinda.

With her nipples now fully extended and her vagina starting to become wet, the Duchess decided to dry down Belinda and move her to the bedroom. Belinda was told to lie down, open her legs wide and masturbate herself in front of the Duchess.
'My Lady, please fuck me as you wish, I know I am your servant, so please use me for your pleasure.' said Belinda.

The Duchess smiled and said, 'Yes servant, I do believe you mean it, and I will test you soon, don't you worry!'

The Duchess left the room and Belinda looked around her. It was a classic motel bedroom, there was nothing to look at which would give her a clue as to where she was. She would just have to wait until the Duchess wanted to have sex with her and perhaps tell her where she was. The Duchess soon returned with two glasses of Gin and Tonic in her hands. She set them down, and started to massage Belinda's long legs. She stretched them out and quickly shackled her ankles to the bottom of the bed with a similar pair of handcuffs Tony had used on her that afternoon in the Maze. This time they were coloured yellow, Belinda wondered idly where they were purchasing them from... Toys Ur Us?

The Duchess started to massage Belinda's arms, it felt so good and she half expected them to be tied to the bedhead but this didn't happen and Belinda soon found out why. They finished their drinks, the Duchess who was also still totally naked, started to massage Belinda's body with her tongue. The Duchess's breasts draped over Belinda's body as she licked her from head to toe. Belinda found it strangely erotic, especially when the Duchess's nipples, now as hard as rivets scraped her soft skin. Belinda responded by rubbing her hand up and down the Duchess's vagina and eventually picked up enough courage to massage her clit.

After some very satisfactory moments according to the loud moans emanating from the Duchess, she stood up and left the room. Belinda started to wonder what she had done wrong, but the Duchess returned with her riding crop in hand. Belinda immediately thought that this was where it was going to get nasty. But being the servant of the Duchess didn't necessarily mean you were going to be whipped into a sexual frenzy. Instead the crop handle was to become a substitute penis. The Duchess smiled at Belinda and said 'Are you ready for this, servant?'

Belinda nodded her head slowly in disbelief, she had read about this type of sexual fantasy, but had never, ever experienced it. Some sales job this was turning out to be! The Duchess wasted no more time and pressed the crop handle into Belinda's vagina. Belinda jumped as she hadn't had really enough foreplay to make her wet enough to receive this size of object. However she grinned and said,
'Thanks My Lady.' She also wickedly thought, 'I must send Jim Stirling one of these.'

Belinda started to grind onto the leather crop handle, in actual real life experiences the handle was smaller than a lot of the cocks she had encountered. The Duchess held it in position and let Belinda enjoy the experience while she sucked her breasts and ate her nipples. The Duchess became more vigorous with the leather crop and Belinda became very wet, orgasming at least three times in quick succession. After some ten minutes the crop was withdrawn and the Duchess licked it all over.

Satisfied, she then walked over to the wardrobe and brought out a strap on penis again made of finest leather. She put it on and entered Belinda in a single thrust. This time Belinda knew she was in for a real hammering and took what felt like an eternity of heavy thrusting, it was truly the best ride she had experienced since the Dutchman Peter Rouse. The Duchess then unlocked Belinda's ankles from their plastic shackles and expertly flipped her onto her front. She started to massage Belinda's back and buttocks.

After a fairly short time the Duchess said to Belinda, 'OK servant it's your turn'. Belinda couldn't believe what she was hearing and watched warily whilst the Duchess removed the straps and put the penis onto Belinda. The Duchess made sure everything was tight and in the right place and slapped Belinda's ass as a gesture of good to go.

Belinda walked around the bedroom with her monster prick out in front of her. She could hardly believe it and happily got to work on the Duchess, first in a standing position, giving it as hard as she had had it all that day. After about seven minutes of pounding the Duchess's vagina and cervix, Belinda asked her to get onto her knees, still remembering to call her 'My Lady'.
'Now hold your tits apart using your nipples My Lady'. Belinda then slid the leather penis up and down between the Duchess's breasts making sure there was a lot of friction taking place. After about five minutes of this technique the Duchess's skin became red and chaffed. 'True justice for keeping me in those plastic handcuffs.' thought Belinda.

In fairness Belinda thought the old bird was not doing too badly, but she didn't let up on the pressure. She had always felt that the British aristocracy needed pain to make any sexual experience worthwhile. She also knew if she didn't give her mistress what she wanted, she would end up back in the cuffs tied to the bed. Belinda entered her vagina again and took her for another five minutes. The Duchess groaned and held her long legs wide for more. 'OK' thought Belinda, 'it's time for a couple of volcanic orgasms' and she entered her mistress's vagina again. The dildo penetrated her cervix whilst stimulating her clitoris and the Duchess quickly orgasmed for her first time.

Belinda kept up the stimulation and soon the Duchess had orgasmed four times. She stammered 'Thank you servant, that was utterly fantastic.' Belinda came out of her and looked at the Duchess's face, she looked totally shattered, her make up was ruined and her immaculate hair was all over the place. Belinda then held her tits hard in her hands and pulled her into an upright position. The Duchess flopped back onto the bed, 'No stamina.' thought Belinda. Then to Belinda's surprise her mistress immediately fell asleep. Belinda had obviously worn her out and suddenly thought what do I do now? She was free to leave, or was she?

Belinda thought for a few moments and an idea entered her head. She took the discarded yellow handcuffs and put them on the Duchess's ankles. The Duchess didn't stir throughout this procedure and was now sleeping very deeply.
'Perfect.' thought Belinda, 'she should stay this way for at least four or five hours which will take me past my twelve hour servant contract'.

The second part of Belinda's plan was simple. As she had arrived at the chalet totally naked she had no clothing and needed something to get back to the Horse and Jockey for her late evening appointment with Peter Rouse. Calmly Belinda went to the wet room and picked up the Duchess's discarded riding clothes and boots. They would fit her just fine and she didn't need to wear the underwear. She quickly pulled on the jodhpurs and riding boots. Standing up she looked at herself in the large mirror... 'Not bad' she thought, 'Indeed they look very sexy', the black boots suited her colouring and the elasticated jodhpurs took the shape of her perfect ass extremely well. She pulled on the white blouse and attached the black cravat around the collar. Lastly she put on the red riding jacket, it indeed was a beauty and must have cost a small fortune. A last look in the mirror told Belinda what she already instinctively knew... she looked a million dollars.

She checked on the now snoring Duchess, grabbed the back riding cap and crop, switched off the lights and left the chalet. As she had hoped the Duchess had left the keys in the ignition. Belinda had no need for the horsebox so she unhooked it and mentally thanked one of her past male flings for teaching her how to caravan. She jumped into the driving seat, started up the engine, put on the headlights and headed for the main road. All she needed now was a signpost to the local town where she could orientate herself, find the Horse and Jockey and keep her appointment with Peter.

Chapter 10;

The Horse and Jockey;

The signposts were true to their word and Belinda soon found her way to the Horse and Jockey. She maneuvered the large car into one of the parking spaces, cut the engine and found her way to reception. It was now 8pm and she asked the youngish man on duty if dinner was still serving.
'There's still twenty more minutes left for orders madam, and might I add how extremely attractive you are looking this evening'. Belinda grinned and wondered if he had recognized the clothes or was just fishing for a bit of sex later on that night, whatever, she didn't want to disappoint so she replied,
'Why thank you, how very gentlemanly of you to say so, especially as I'm dining alone!'
He smiled in return and nodded slowly as if confirming he might be available that evening.

'Please book me in for dinner, I'll be down in ten minutes.'
'Certainly Madam.'
Belinda asked for her key and went immediately to her room, she quickly spruced herself up and viewed the mirror. Yes she agreed, I do look extremely attractive in a very raw sexy way in this riding gear. I think this is a must new style for me, hopefully Peter Rouse will feel the same.

However there was no time to lose, she was famished, she hadn't eaten since that very quick lunchtime BBQ and she needed strength for the rest of what was going to be a very active evening. She ran down to the dining room, got shown her table and immediately ordered a bottle of Chardonnay, Chilean of course. Belinda prided herself on knowing her wines, her father after all was a sales manager for one of the big wine cellars in central London and he had spent many evenings training her in one of the best sales techniques for getting clients to buy without remorse. Drinking very good wine... and lots of it!

Belinda dined at her leisure and for the first time that day she felt she wasn't under pressure, though her strange clothing didn't fit all that well and made her feel quite hot. She couldn't wait to start removing some of it she thought wickedly. Her meal finished Belinda took the rest of her wine to her room in an ice bucket where she sipped it slowly.

It was now 11.00pm and it was time for Peter to make an appearance. Belinda went down to the lobby where she ordered another bottle of Chardonnay, popped it into the replenished ice bucket and waited for Peter. Spot on at 11.30 he walked through the lobby door and saw Belinda immediately. He opened his hands and kissed her on the cheek, both sides...not unusual for a sophisticated European.
'Would you like a drink Mr. Rouse?
'Oh please keep calling me Peter, after all we are very much acquainted after this afternoons events. Have I told you, you have a wonderful body my dear, and much, much better without the mud!'
They both laughed and Peter said,

'I do like your current outfit Belinda... very much in tune with this hotel'.

Belinda gently blushed, she couldn't tell him how she had acquired the clothing, and she really did enjoy wearing it.
'I do like wearing adventurous garments Peter and I hoped these would tweak your interest!'
'Top marks! Is that what they say in the show jumping circles?'
Belinda replied quickly,
'I'm more of a fox chasing type of person myself!'
'Ha ha ha... very good Belinda, I do enjoy your style of humour... now let's have some of that delicious wine.'

Belinda poured Peter a glass and leant back on the leather settee. Peter sat beside her and gently fondled her left thigh. Belinda decided to get round to business quickly, before she lost her tentative female advantage.
'Peter, could we position some of our pots and pans range in your supermarkets?'
'Absolutely', Peter replied, 'In fact this afternoon we've just ordered 3000 units of your Oxy Brillo range to get you started, and my purchasing team are looking at other products of yours which will fit into our present range of kitchen utensils.
'Wow!' Belinda gasped and opened her legs slightly.

Peter quickly took advantage and moved his hand higher up her thigh. Belinda undid her cravat and slowly unbuttoned the top four of her shirt buttons. Her delicious cleavage was now on view. Peter quickly moved his other hand to fondle her left breast and rubbed the nipple showing through the white linen.
'No problem Belinda, after all your company's products are top class, if a little expensive and I'm sure we can overcome that little problem between us.'

'Yes!' Belinda gasped, her senses working overtime between Peter's massaging her very upper thigh and breast.
'I have access to some marketing incentives which will help.'
'Shhh, Belinda, just relax,' said Peter, 'we can discuss this all at the office next week in Amsterdam when you come to visit me.'
'Am I?' replied Belinda, 'Oh yes of course, I really can't wait!'
'Well let's make it Thursday, OK?'
'Yes, yes, I'll be there.'

'But now,' said Peter, let's get down to some real business.'
He slowly unbuttoned the remaining buttons on Belinda's shirt and let her full oval breasts fall out. In one fluid movement he tucked her shirt into the back of her jodhpurs and started kissing her. Belinda groaned, she could never resist the soft male touch of a mouth on her nipples, and Peter was exquisite in his sensuality.

Above his head in the corner of the lobby Belinda noticed a red light blinking... it was a security camera, no doubt recording what was going on. Her mind thought of the young man behind the desk when she checked in... yes that was it, he was building his profile of her for his personal use. A wicked thought entered her mind, she would give him a session o record, and Peter Rouse a very good time into the bargain.

Chapter 11;

Sunday Night 11.55pm;

Belinda groaned more loudly,
'Peter, that's so good, would you mind removing my riding jacket and shirt?'
Peter was already feeling randy and he promptly striped Belinda of her upper garments. He folded them neatly, and placed the already discarded cravat on top of them on a nearby table. The lobby was very quiet, Sunday night at just about midnight meant the clients had all retired to bed, he felt he had a free rein to do what he needed to do.

'Massage me.' continued Belinda 'My tits so need a good massage.' Peter acquiesced and concentrated his hands on her upper body. It was a firm body with lots of good muscle and superb rock hard nipples, he thought to himself, she'll need these nipples if she's going to make the sales she wants. Belinda groaned more loudly and watched the movement of the camera and its blinking red light out of the corner of her eye.

'Peter, strip me, I so need to feel your hand on my clitoris, handle my cervix hard.' Again Peter acquiesced and gently pulled down the jodhpurs to the top of Belinda's black leather riding boots.
'No,' Belinda gasped, 'everything... take off the riding boots.' Peter took his hands off her jodhpurs and pulled first at her left boot and then her right boot. With both successfully removed it only took a second to pull the jodhpurs off Belinda's body.

At last he had her completely naked lying in front of him on the hotel lobby leather sofa. Belinda slowly moved her legs apart showing him her seductive vagina and all the mysteries he was about to again discover.
'Pass me my glass of Chardonnay.' Belinda drank it all in one go and calmly poured the remaining few drops over her vagina. She rubbed the golden liquid into her soft tanned flesh and beckoned Peter to taste it. Behind his head Belinda observed the camera recording the event.

Peter Rouse was no mean artist when it came to sexual activity, but never before had he been so completely entranced by such a beautiful female. He had no doubt in his own mind that he had come here to seduce her but this one was different, could he have met his equal in his sexual symbolic world? He shook his head, there was no way this girl was not his equal, she was better than all the others, he had to stick to his plan and attempt to make himself dominant over her. But he couldn't do it in a public hotel lobby, he needed a private room away from prying people and no doubt hidden security cameras.

After five or six minutes of massaging Belinda's clitoris with his tongue he tasted the first orgasm Belinda had that night. It was so sweet, yet bitter. As an aphrodisiac he needed nothing else... except complete privacy. Belinda was now moaning consistently and Peter, still fully clothed, continued to massage her vagina and breast nipples. Each in their turn... and making sure to never let the sexual pressure he had now so carefully built decline.

At last he had had enough,
'Belinda, I want you, I want all your body with my body and we need to retire to your room.'
'Peter, I thought you'd never ask.' replied Belinda winking at the silent camera.

They both slowly stood up and realized Belinda was completely naked and Peter was completely dressed.
'We must look completely stupid.' Peter exclaimed.
Belinda burst out laughing and said, 'Pass me my riding jacket and boots'. She put on the jacket which neatly covered up her breasts and then pulled on both leather riding boots which hid nothing except her lower legs and toes.
'Very daring!' said Peter with a laugh and collected the unfinished wine in its ice bucket.

Walking past the reception area, Peter asked Belinda if she would like a nightcap as well as another bottle of wine. They both decided on brandy and the youngish man behind reception poured the golden liquid into two impeccable glasses. He said he would bring up the wine to Belinda's room as soon as he located some more ice. Peter now carrying both glasses of the swirling golden brown liquid followed Belinda's seductively swaying ass up the main staircase to her room.

Once inside, Belinda immediately removed her red jacket and asked Peter to do the honours with her riding boots.
'Have a sip first my dear, it's too good to delay any longer.' Belinda sat down on the edge of the bed and sipped her brandy.
'Besides, I'd like to fuck you with your boots on... they're extremely sexual in their own way you know!'
Belinda murmured 'If only you knew their origins.' and lay back on the bed anticipating Peter's desire.

It only took Peter Rouse twenty five seconds to remove his clothes and position himself beside Belinda on the bed, he grabbed her cervix, his penis was already well aroused and Belinda knew it would only take a little bit of extra encouragement to make it rock solid. She started to massage his chest, concentrating on his nipples. She then dipped her right forefinger into her brandy glass and rubbed it onto his upper body making a delicate figure of eight in a clockwise motion over his stomach. Peter relaxed, lay on his back and let Belinda's tongue follow the pattern of the brandy.

His cock shuddered and Belinda lifted herself onto it. Slowly, slowly she went down on his hard penis and when she felt it had fully entered her she started to grind her pubic bone against his. Peter started to groan in time to her motion, his voice became more intense as Belinda increased the friction between their two bodies. Within a minute he orgasmed and white semen came trickling out of Belinda's vagina.

Belinda immediately caught the escaping liquid with her forefinger and once again traced the figure of eight pattern onto Peter's abdomen. He groaned more deeply and cried out as if in torment,
'More, more, more... Belinda!

'Sshhh, my darling Peter, you will get as much as you need, trust me!

Belinda continued the deep sexual movement until Peter again orgasmed, this time very deeply. Within seconds he had fallen unconscious, deeply asleep and Belinda withdrew her vagina knowing she had hit the target.

It took Peter Rouse one complete hour to wake up and when he did he felt as if he had shed twenty years of his life. He felt so energetic, so composed, so fulfilled. He looked around the hotel bedroom until he saw the naked Belinda, sitting on a casual chair watching him wake up.
'Belinda, Belinda,' he stammered, 'that was stupendous, I feel so very good, so very alive, what did you do to me?'
"Peter, we just had good old fashioned sex... it was what we both wanted, and when you get what you want, you feel great!'

Peter nodded slowly, as if realizing he had missed something important, but couldn't just quite remember what it was.
'Ok, but thank you, very, very much.'
'Peter, it's all my pleasure and thank you for your business order.'
'Belinda, it's nothing, but could you excuse me, I do need to get back to my wife, we both didn't expect me to be out for so long.'

Belinda smiled and said, 'Peter that's no problem, I'll see you Thursday afternoon in your Amsterdam offices.'
'That's a date.' He replied, 'I'm so looking forward to it, but you must experience Amsterdam at night and we'll get you back to London on the late afternoon Friday flight.'
'I'll make the arrangements and bring some evening wear.'
'Not too much, Belinda, not too much.' said Peter as he let himself out of the room.

Chapter 12;

The Night Receptionist;

Belinda put on her riding jacket, jodhpurs and leather boots, sat down in the corner chair and slowly sipped the rest of her unfinished brandy. Sure enough five minutes later there was a knock on her door.
'Room service, Madam.'
'Come in please.'

The youngish man on reception entered the room with a trolley on which sat the ice bucket with a full bottle of Chilean Chardonnay. Beside it sat two rounds of what looked like turkey sandwiches, one of Belinda's many favourite late night snacks

'My sincere apologies for the lateness of the hour, but the ice machine started to play up Madam.'
'I'm sure it did young man, don't apologise, your timing is appropriate, and I hope it's not the first time tonight it will be so!' It took about thirty seconds for the receptionist to understand Belinda's remark and he burst into a wide grin.
'I understand Madam, thank you.' With that he shut the door, walked over to Belinda and kissed her on the lips.

Belinda took his head in her left hand and returned the kiss with a similar vigour. He put his hands around her waist and pulled her body into his. She could feel his cock throbbing with excitement as they drew closer, but she did feel a tad hungry after her couple of hours with Peter. Slowly she let him go and said,
'It would be a pity to waste such a good wine and these wonderful sandwiches... have you eaten tonight?'
'In actual fact I haven't.' he replied, 'I tend to satisfy my sexual appetite first and then eat.'
'Well in that case I think we'll break the rules just a little, here and now.' Belinda reached over and took a sandwich, at the same time she unbuttoned the only single button on her riding jacket. Her breasts once again fell out and stayed on show whilst she finished the sandwich. The youngish man took one as well and poured them both a glass of wine.

He sat on the edge of the bed and announced,
'You can't beat the high life!' Belinda laughed and toasted him with her half empty glass. One sandwich was enough for Belinda and she removed her riding jacket. She watched the instantaneous response in the youngish man's trousers and asked him to remove them. He obliged, but also took off his shirt, pants, shoes and socks. Now standing naked before her, she called him over. Belinda took his erect penis and gently rubbed cold chardonnay onto it. In fairness to the youngish man he didn't flinch and Belinda put his cock between her breasts. Using her two hands she squeezed both breasts together tightly and started to masturbate his penis.

It only took half a minute for him to start groaning. His hands fondled her long black hair bringing it up to the top of her head and letting it fall time after time. However to Belinda's surprise he didn't ejaculate and she guessed she'd have to work a bit harder to get that result.

'Would you mind removing my riding boots... it enables me to pull down my jodhpurs you see.' He nodded understanding immediately and helped pull them off Belinda's legs and feet. By now Belinda had lost count of the times she had pulled on or pulled off these riding boots in the past ten hours, but she thought they were getting more supple each time. Perhaps like her own body she mused.

'Ravish me!' she commanded the youngish man, and he immediately removed her jodhpurs. Now naked he followed the black line of pubic hair to Belinda's vaginal region. He got down on his knees, pushed her legs apart and gently started probing her clitoris with his tongue. Belinda once again that evening groaned softly at the foreign invasion of her pubic area. But this time it was different she thought, this unexpected pleasure was for her and her only... a perfect way to end a busy working day. No business deals, no reputations to be lost or offended, just a plain simple fucking session.

Chapter 13;

The Duchess comes clean;

It was six thirty in the morning when Belinda awoke from her deep sleep. The receptionist had left at two thirty giving her a much needed four hours sleep. There was much to do and certainly no time for breakfast, even if it were being served by the very sexually fulfilled night receptionist called Sam.

This time Belinda dressed in one of her simple one piece, black, work dresses with matching lace bra and panties. Her plan was very simple. She would get back to the motel, release the Duchesses ankles from the yellow handcuffs, take her back to the chairman's house where she could collect her company car and get into work for nine. The Duchess could then collect her trailer from the motel and continue her sex life as she wanted... but without her involvement. Belinda would also reluctantly return the horse riding outfit which had served her extremely well all Sunday evening.

The traffic was nonexistent as she left the Horse and Jockey. Sam had obviously gone to kitchen duty so no time was lost in saying farewell. The company was picking up the tab on the overnight room and meals, so she got off to a good start. She quickly motored through the beautiful Oxfordshire countryside to the Motel where she had left the Duchess attached to her bed. The horsebox was still in the parking spot where she had left it and the motel room looked quiet.

Belinda jumped out of the big vehicle and entered the room. In the bedroom she found the Duchess where she had left her, albeit her make up now smeared to hell.
Belinda switched off the bedside light and gently shook the Duchess awake.
'You've come back to release me.' was the first words she murmured.
'Yes.' said Belinda equally as softly, 'But you must understand that as I was your sex servant, so now you are mine.'
The Duchess started to sob softly and replied,
I always knew it would come to this, I have to tell you, I was a very reluctant player in this erotic game, they left me no choice in the end, and now here I am... a sex servant to you, Miss Belinda.'

Belinda blinked, was this whole episode a game organized by someone else, was there a master planner behind all of the tombola activities and the ramifications they were producing. It certainly couldn't be coincidence that she, Bella and Giselle were the ones to be made servants. Perhaps the Duchess knew more than she was telling, she needed to proceed softly, she needed the Duchess on her side.

If you can call me Miss Belinda then I can happily call you 'My Lady'. Is this a good start to an equal relationship between us?'

'I think so, yes I know so... oh how I do want to be a sexual servant to you Miss Belinda! I just want you to fuck me hard with my beautiful black leather dildo and respect me for what I am... a happy sex servant to you!'
'Well that's fine I suppose, from your perspective, but what do I get out of the relationship.' replied Belinda.

The Duchess thought for a moment.
'I know that sexually I'm a bit over the top, age wise that is, but I do assure you I am a fanatical lover, and in my role as your sex servant I will do your every bidding. I am open to all new sex erotica and I promise to never disobey you in the sexual act. I will drink your orgasms, and eat your vagina all day long until you order me to stop.'
Belinda quickly interrupted and said,
'I get your intentions, and they are truly what I need of you if you wish to become my sex servant. But surely a person as well connected to the lineage of Britain, I mean you being a Duchess with all what that means, could surely open doors I couldn't dream of ever even encountering.'
'Miss Belinda, I adore you so much, yes, I will be able to introduce you into the highest sexual circles in the land.'

Belinda bent over and pulled the plastic handcuffs off the Duchesses ankles. The Duchess stood up and stretched her cramped body. Her nipples hardened with her feeling of freedom and they were now as large as the three inch rivets which had held the hull of the fateful Titanic together. Belinda was drawn to them like a magnet, she needed to touch them, caress them and finally suck them. The Duchess stood still as Belinda fulfilled her desires.

After two minutes of caressing and sucking, the Duchess carefully removed Belinda's one piece black work dress. She then slowly removed her black lace bra and after a few moments her panties. Belinda stepped out of her high heels and guided the Duchess back to the bed.

Chapter 14;

Monday Morning 7.45am

'My Lady, I feel I need to fulfill your strongest desires.'
'Yes, Miss Belinda, please do what you need to me, and then if you so desire please fuck me with the black leather dildo, hard, up my vagina and don't stop... if it pleases you, Miss Belinda.'

'My Lady, it does please me and I shall fulfill your needs, but then you need to drive me back to my car so I can get to work and end this very strange weekend.'
'Yes, I accept your terms, please buckle on the dildo and fuck me slowly... Miss Belinda.'

Belinda walked over to the closet and took out the dildo. She carefully strapped it on making sure it was tight around her ass. The leather straps and chrome buckles took the strain and the dildo was ready for action. The Duchess smiled and opened her legs wide as she lay back on the bed and let Belinda enter her slowly. Belinda lowered her head, her long black hair fell over the Duchesses breasts, she found the still extended nipples and started to chew them gently as she increased the friction on the Duchess's clitoris.

A low moan came from the bed, which increased in intensity as the two females maintained their rhythm; the Dildo was strapped on so tightly that Belinda felt its surging movement hit her pubic area each time she penetrated further into the Duchess. Meanwhile the Duchess had found Belinda's tits and was massaging her nipples as strongly as Belinda was chewing her own. The Duchess suddenly climaxed, her orgasm was even more infectious on Belinda, and she pushed the dildo harder into her cervix. Eventually Belinda came out as gently as she could, realigned the dildo and went in again. The Duchess steadied herself and let out a long sigh as the dildo hit her ovaries. Belinda pushed it further and further into her vagina, she leant forward and sucked the Duchess's tits and again started to ride her, hard.

'Please don't stop Miss Belinda, this is so good! The Duchess cried out in ecstasy.
'Yes My Lady... even I'm enjoying it, and soon it's going to be even better!'
Belinda had no idea how what she was doing was going to improve, but she was up for it for at least another ten minutes. The Duchess lasted only two minutes when she orgasmed and Belinda felt it was time to change tack. By now she herself was feeling extremely horny and standing up she unbuckled the dildo and threw it onto the floor.
"OK My Lady, it's your turn to please me... suck me all over!'

Belinda lay down on the bed as the Duchess got onto her knees. Needing no further instruction the Duchess started to lick Belinda's breasts, her tongue snaked down to her pubic hair and followed the trail to her vagina. Meanwhile Belinda grabbed her servant's ample tits and started to rub them hard. The Duchess groaned, Belinda groaned as her clit started to be punished by the Duchess's tongue. A few minutes later, Belinda orgasmed, not once but twice, her mind went into turmoil, the deep sensations were too much for her. She struggled to regain consciousness and all she could murmur was,

'Thank you My Lady, thank you My Lady.'

'Thank you Miss Belinda.' Was the only reply she received as the Duchess got up and went to the closet. 'It's time we finished this crazy weekend so let's get back to our real lives before we're missed!'
'I agree, but what are you looking for?' replied Belinda.
'My riding gear… I know I had it with me, but don't worry, I've got my white linen suit right here… I'll wear that instead, the midday meeting at the Jockey Club doesn't require any formal wear… unless it's a dinner of course! She laughed and Belinda joined in, totally unaware of the etiquette of horse riding circles.

Belinda and the Duchess showered separately, then dressed and prepared themselves for the day. While Belinda hooked up the horse box to the 4x4 the Duchess packed the leather dildo safely into its special zinc coated case, much like a professional photographer's camera. With the motel room cleared, the Duchess locked the door, left the keys at reception and started the engine of the big vehicle. In fairness she only scuffed one corner on the journey back to the country house where Belinda's Merc was parked.

Belinda jumped out of the front passenger seat and said farewell to the Duchess. They had swopped email addresses and planned a reunion at a hotel on the Isle of Whyte in three weeks' time. It was a gala ball and the Duchess had promised to introduce her 'Sexual Mistress' to some new acquaintances. Belinda took out her car keys and opened the Merc. It started first time, she waved goodbye to the Duchess, who promptly accelerated off in a cloud of gravel and dust.

Belinda lost no time in following her and was in the office for a very respectable 9.30am. As she sat down at her desk, Belinda could only wonder what the next two weeks would hold for her, if they were anything like the last 24 hours, she would be truly fucked!

The End;

If you enjoyed Belinda Blinked 1; then Belinda Blinked 2; will immerse you deeper into Belinda's sexual world of big business and the rich aristocracy... I promise! Rocky xx.

Hey... still hungry for more then why not let me send you some exclusive Belinda material. I've got some stuff which I didn't have room for in this book and you're welcome to read it. I also sometimes send out a newsletter with info about the main characters, a new book or podcast. It'll keep you up to date on Belinda's activities and whet your appetite for more! It's easy, just email me at flintstonerocky@gmail.com and I'll get back to you.

So this is what you get;

1. Material that didn't make this book.
2. A copy of Belinda's payslip.
3. An occasional newsletter.
4. Advance notice of what's happening in Belinda's world!

Myself, Belinda, Giselle, Bella and Tony would love you to leave us an honest review. It really helps us to maintain our success in the book rankings. Thank you!

If you haven't yet read Belinda Blinked 1 or 2, then just Google it!
You can find us at
www.BelindaBlinked.com
and
www.RockyFlintstone.com

Printed in Great Britain
by Amazon